TREES OF THE SPIRIT

HIGHERLIFE
PUBLISHING & MARKETING

About the Author

Travis English has a passion for writing children's books that provide proactive strategies for defining, teaching, and supporting positive and appropriate student behaviors.

As a former substitute teacher, Travis believes that value-based learning is essential to character and social development in children. His unique writing style is rooted in hip-hop and classical poetry. Travis' rhyme, flow, and conceptual themes are all crucial factors in creating compelling content for children.

englishdialect.co for more!

A Special Thanks to Illustrators

Carolyn English, Robert Morris, and Molly Wu

**This project would not have been possible
without your creativity and dedication.**

THANK YOU!

Trees of the Spirit
Copyright © 2021 by Travis English
Published by HigherLife Publishing and Marketing
All Rights Reserved solely by the author
ISBN 978-1-954533-93-6

There once were some children from a land far away.

And in this place, life was beautiful—such a fun chance to play.

There was never any darkness, only bright days.

But as time went on the people grew cold.

And many new problems began to unfold.

From early in the morning, until late in the night

the leaders would bicker about left versus right.

They fought about the color for the town's fences.

As if brown or white made any difference.

4

Then came break-ins and protests and times of violence.

Plus, all these incidents stemmed from hate and defiance.

Thus, the fighting continued by those who were foolish.

What was once a nice town was now full of anguish.

So, when summer arrived several children went West

to visit their grandpa and escape the mess.

Their grandpa's house was cozy and built on a farm.

There were gobs of cool trees and a little red barn.

The children climbed the trees all the way to the top

and picked all the fruit that never seemed to drop.

8

There were plums, oranges, and grapes all enormous!

Lemons, persimmons, and figs that were gorgeous!

Plus, over on the hill watched several white horses.

Which Grandpa said, "Were angelic forces."

"My orchard is home to the Trees of the Spirit,

and their message is useful to those who hear it."

So, the curious children followed Grandpa around.

To learn from the trees and explore the lush grounds.

12

The first tree was huge and contained lots of fruit!

It believed in all things and hoped for them too.

It survived every storm that Mother Nature discharged,

and cast out all fear because its trunk was so large.

♥

This tree was called Love for it endured throughout time.

Love was unconditional—whether watered or dry.

It was the greatest of the trees, its branches so wide.

The children were amazed at Love's wonderful size.

14

Next came a trumpet tree that could not be contained.

Its name was Joy, and it sang unashamed!

It was blissful in nature and made the children laugh,

and urged them not to give up when trials crossed their path.

Joy was radiant with beauty and free from despair.

Its branches offered relief for everyone to share.

Around the bend was a tree that surpassed all understanding.

It never felt anxious because it was firm and undoubting.

There was freedom in its presence. It was quiet and restful.

Grandpa called this tree Peace; its benefits were exceptional!

Peace always smiled, painting a sunset in the sky,

and its leaves blew in the breeze with its head held high.

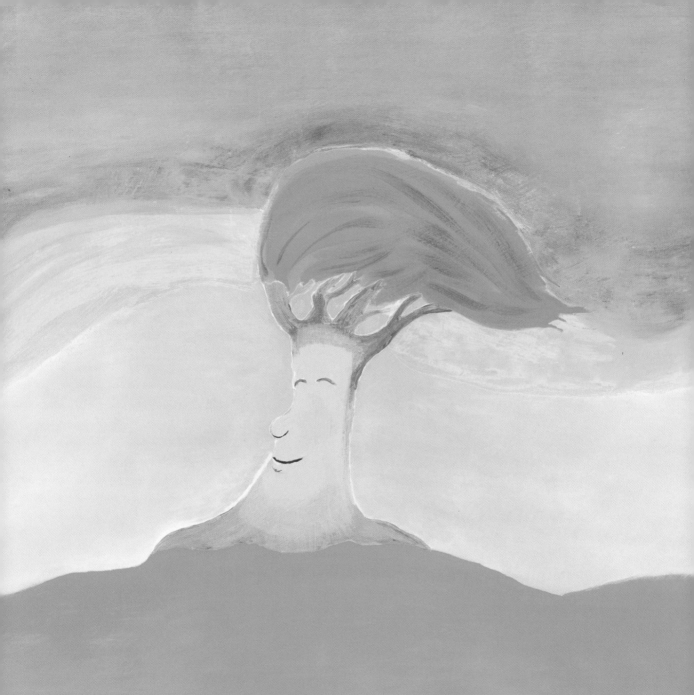

The following tree was surrounded by weeds!

But its composure was evident by calmness indeed.

It learned restraint as a sapling in youth,

and it never grew weary of living its truth.

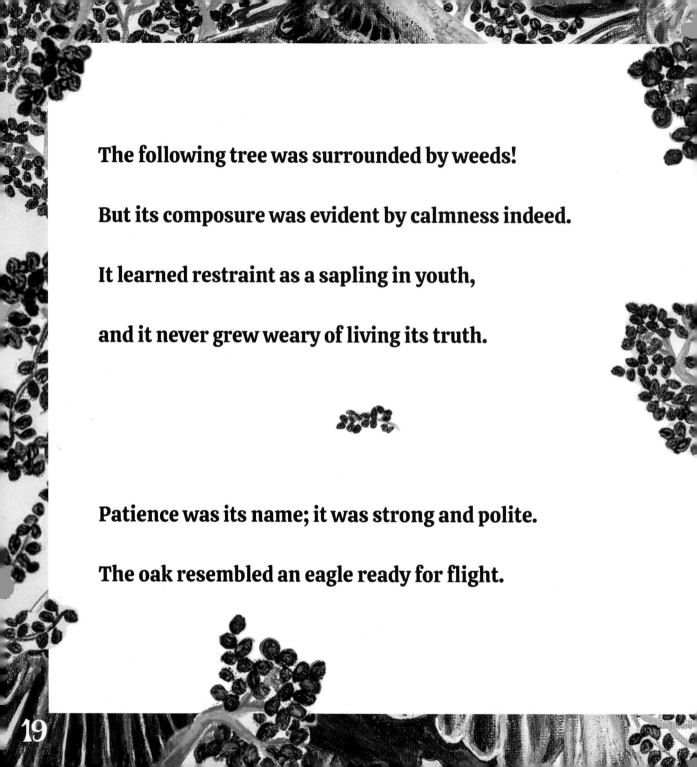

Patience was its name; it was strong and polite.

The oak resembled an eagle ready for flight.

In the middle of the orchard was a very special breed,

a tree that always lent a branch to someone in need.

It was generous and forgiving from one to another,

and it truly cared for its sisters and brothers.

*

This tree, called Kindness, was considerate and fair.

Grandpa told the children that its fruit was most rare.

Up on a hill, stood a tree dependable and tall.

But that wasn't enough, so it showed good deeds to all.

This tree was called Goodness and it made all things better.

Plus, there were doves in its branches with pretty white feathers!

Goodness was generous and enjoyed their company;

it showered them each with candy that tasted like honey.

As they continued, they reached Grandpa's oldest friend:

the tree of Faith on which all could depend.

The children were astonished by this tree in all its might,

for it had no eyes, but by Faith it had sight.

It was confident and hopeful from beginning to end.

Through belief and resolve, it continued to ascend!

Instead of fruit, Faith gave the children a mustard seed,

which would help them move mountains in times of need.

Then there was a tree that was humble and pure.

Its name was Meekness, and it had the world's cure.

It always put others before its own needs,

and everywhere it went it tried to sow seeds.

Meekness told the kids, "Don't forget where you're from."

Then it pulled up some roots and offered them some.

The roots were shiny and magical in their hands!

When the children ate them—they inherited the land!

The last tree in the orchard, Self-Control, was truly a giant!

It was steadfast, loyal, and roared like a lion!

It never got flustered by the birds in its branches,

and wasn't affected by the squirrels and their stashes.

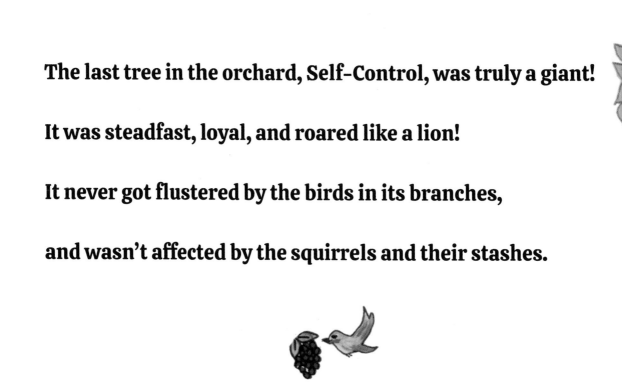

Self-control was a wise tree, taking years to reach size.

Though its fruit was amazing, like a supernatural prize!

30

When the children left the orchard and headed for home.

They could not believe how much they had grown.

Their grandpa was joyful and everyone could hear it.

His grandkids had just learned from The Trees of the Spirit!

So, the children returned to the land that was ruined,

bringing what they learned, teaching truth like good stewards.

The leaders of the town could not believe their own ears.

The Trees of the Spirit brought grown men to tears.

Slowly but surely the town returned to peace,

and the children became leaders in the land of the free!

So, remember this story! I will even say please.

When you struggle in life...

Remember The Trees.

36

English Dialect

englishdialect.co